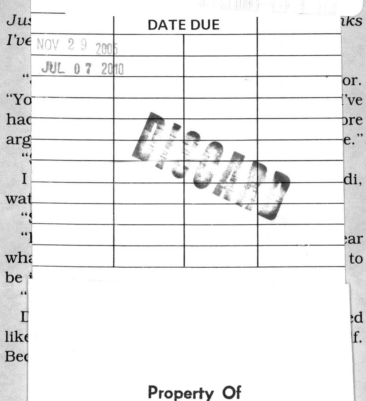

Jus *ks*
I've NOV 2 9 2005
JUL 0 7 2010

" or.
"Yo 've
had re
arg e."
"

I di,
wat

"

"I ar
wha to
be

"

D ed
like f.
Bec

Look for these and other books in THE GYMNASTS series:

THE GYMNASTS

#7 TUMBLING GHOSTS

Elizabeth Levy

AN
APPLE
PAPERBACK

Property Of
Pittsford Public Library

SCHOLASTIC INC.
New York Toronto London Auckland Sydney

ISBN 0-590-42221-9

Copyright © 1989 by Elizabeth Levy. All rights reserved. Published by Scholastic Inc. APPLE PAPERBACKS is a registered trademark of Scholastic Inc. THE GYMNASTS is a trademark of Scholastic Inc.

12 11 10 9 8 7 6 5 4 3 2 1   9/8 0 1 2 3 4/9

Printed in the U.S.A.   28

First Scholastic printing, September 1989

To Alisa Malinovich.
Thanks for the great idea.

Wicked Witch of
the Middle West

I'm Irish-American. People always say the Irish have a temper. I wish I could say, "Not me," but I can't. I lose my cool all the time. My good friends, the other Pinecones, say, "Jodi, it's not so bad — at least we know what you're thinking." But I've got to tell the truth: My temper gets me in trouble.

Lauren Baca, Darlene Broderick, Cindi Jockett, and I all started at Patrick's Evergreen Gymnastics Academy together. The Pinecones are my team. The four of us think of ourselves as the original Pinecones. Everybody always expects me to be an outstanding gymnast because I was almost born into gymnastics. My mom was great as a competitor, and now she's an assistant coach at the Evergreen Academy. Before my mom and dad got divorced they used to run their own gym back in St. Louis. But the truth is that I'm not that good. Mom and Dad didn't want to push me, and it's only since working with Patrick that I take gymnastics seriously at all. Or at least a little seriously.

Becky Dyson is my least favorite gymnast at Patrick's. When I mentioned my temper, I was thinking about Becky. She always gets my goat.

Becky's a better gymnast than any of the Pinecones, and she never lets us forget it. Luckily she's not a Pinecone. She's in the more advanced group, but a week ago she pulled a muscle and she's just coming back from her injury. Patrick has her working out with us for a little while. He thought having Becky in our group would inspire us. It almost did . . . to murder. Becky never has a nice thing to say about *anyone* other than herself, and she seems to take particular pleasure in putting *me* down. Thank goodness, after Halloween she'll be back up where she belongs — in the rafters, if you ask me.

It was the middle of October, and I was psyched. Halloween is just about my favorite holiday.

"Jodi, what are you going to be for Halloween?" Ti An asked me as we sat down on the mats to begin our warm-ups for gymnastics class. We began with some simple stretches. Ti An is the youngest Pinecone. She joined after Darlene and everyone else.

"I can't decide between a mummy and a vampire," I said.

"Go for the mummy," said Lauren, giggling. "I'd like to see you all wrapped up."

"I'll wrap *you* in aluminum foil. You can come as a baked potato," I said. Lauren loves food.

"That's not a bad idea," said Lauren.

"Aren't we a little too old for Halloween?" asked Ashley. Ashley is all of nine, but I think she was born middle-aged. She's a first-class pill.

"Come off it," I argued. "We're just eleven. Ti An's only eight. My older sister still gets dressed up for Halloween and she's at the Air Force Academy."

"What does she go as, an astronaut?" asked Lauren.

"Last year she went as a jar of mustard," I said.

Lauren giggled. "Maybe I'll go as a hot dog."

"I love Halloween," said Darlene, who's thirteen and the oldest of the Pinecones. "This year I want to go as a Bronco cowgirl cheerleader."

"You won't have any trouble getting the costume," said Cindi. Darlene's dad is "Big Beef" Broderick, a linebacker for the Denver Broncos.

"Girls," said Patrick. "I don't mind a little chit-chat during warm-ups, but let's keep it down."

"We could go as the Pinecone pretzels," I said, as I put my leg behind my head. I'm a little bit double-jointed.

Patrick laughed. "Could I have a little less talk and a little more concentration on your stretches?"

We did our backbends. Cindi collapsed next to me. She rolled over on her stomach. "What *are* we doing for Halloween?" she asked.

I liked the way she said "we." When I first moved here from St. Louis, I worried about feeling left out. Cindi and Lauren were already best friends, and Darlene was practically famous. I didn't know where I would fit in. But the Pinecones have turned out to be the best thing that ever happened to me.

"When I was in St. Louis we had the best Halloweens in the world," I said.

"Spare me," said Becky. "I can't imagine anything more boring than Halloween in St. Louis."

"A lot *you* know," I said. "Halloween there was something incredible. It was just for gymnasts."

"I bet they voted you Wicked Witch of the Middle West," whispered Becky, too softly for Patrick to hear.

"You're the wicked witch!" I snapped.

4

"Jodi," warned Patrick. "Watch your temper."

"Me?" I exclaimed. "Becky's the one who called me a wicked witch."

Ashley giggled. Ashley giggles at everything Becky says. Ashley is also a Pinecone. Personally I think she's more of a conehead, especially for looking up to Becky, but Ashley doesn't ask my opinion. In fact, I'll bet I'm the Pinecone that Becky and Ashley like the least.

"Wicked Witch of the Middle West," repeated Ashley.

"Becky, you're the one who would make the perfect witch," said Lauren.

"I'll get you for that," barked Becky.

"Girls," said Patrick sharply. "I asked you to warm up, not sharpen your claws."

"You know," I said, "we really should do what we did in St. Louis. Patrick, you'll love this. It was such a blast!"

"I'd like to blast Jodi into outer space on a broomstick," said Becky. "If that cretin says one more word about Halloween in St. Louis, I'll barf."

"Becky," warned Patrick, "cut it out. And Jodi, a little more concentration on your warm-up would be nice. If you girls have so much energy for sniping at each other today, let's use it to do some stomach crunches."

"Don't you want to hear what my idea is?" I begged. I'll do anything to get out of stomach crunches.

"Jodi," said Patrick, laughing at me, "sometimes your mind outraces your mouth. Okay, what did you do?"

I sat up on the mat. I loved being the center of attention. "Listen up, everybody," I said. "When we were in St. Louis we had an all-night Halloween party in the gym," I explained. "We decorated the place like a haunted house, and all the gymnasts got to spend the night in the gym. We slept on the mats. It was so much fun — a blast!"

"Oh, oh . . . it sounds too thrilling for words," said Becky, mocking me.

"I think it sounds like fun," said Darlene.

"It sounds excruciatingly boring," said Becky. "Who wants to spend the night with a group of Pinecones? It's bad enough that I'm spending this week with them."

"Becky!" warned Patrick. "The Pinecones are a valuable part of the academy. Just because you're a notch above them as a gymnast, doesn't give you the right to lord it over them. You could learn a lot about teamwork from them."

I stuck my tongue out at Becky. Infantile, I admit. But fun. Luckily Patrick didn't see me.

"I think a Halloween party in the gym sounds

neat," said Ti An. "I've never spent all night in a gym."

"I think it sounds super," said Lauren.

"Well, if you don't stop talking about it and finish your warm-ups, you'll *all* spend tonight in the gym," said Patrick.

"What a bunch of dweebs!" said Becky.

"Please, Patrick," I begged, ignoring Becky. "Doesn't it sound terrific?"

"It's intriguing, I admit," said Patrick. "But I'm a little swamped right now. I'm not sure I have time to organize it. Halloween is coming up fast."

"What's to organize?" I argued. "We come in costume, we play and eat, we get to haunt the gym. . . ." I waved my hands in Ti An's face, pretending to haunt her. I started to tickle her. "The tickle monster will show up."

Ti An shrieked.

Patrick shook his head. "I have a feeling there'll be a lot more work than that. Let me think about it. In the meantime, do you think you could get your minds off Halloween and do a little gymnastics?"

"How about levitating witches?" I said as I got up from the mats.

"Back-flipping goblins?" said Lauren.

"How about we go over your beam routine?" said Patrick. "How about being perfect Pinecones on the beam?"

"There's no such thing," said Becky.

"Seriously, Patrick, do you think we can have the Halloween party?" I asked.

Patrick patted the beam. "Get up here, Jodi. I told you I'd think about it. For now, let's think about gymnastics."

2

An Orphan on Halloween Night

A couple of days went by, and Patrick still hadn't mentioned the Halloween party. I had a feeling he wasn't going to let us do it.

We were working on our tumbling. "Roundoff to back-handspring!" shouted Patrick, clapping his hands. I love tumbling. It's fast, and you don't have to think too much, like you do on the beam or the uneven bars.

"I'm ready, Patrick!" I shouted.

Patrick got set to spot me. "I'm not going to foul up this time," I said. "I don't need a spot. Don't worry. I can do it alone. Let me do it alone."

"Slow down, Jodi," Patrick warned me. "Remember, take your time." I was puzzled. The whole point of a tumbling run is that it's a run. It happens fast.

"What do you mean 'slow down'?" I asked. "I'll never make the handspring if I slow down. It doesn't make sense," I said.

"You have to slow down your internal clock," said Patrick. "It's the secret of real explosive power in gymnastics. Explosive power doesn't come just from strength. It comes from your head."

Sometimes when Patrick tries to explain to me *how* to do something, he just makes it sound more complicated and I get really baffled. "Can't I just *do* it? If I think too much about it, I get confused," I whined.

"*I* understand what Patrick means," said Ashley, who was standing behind me in line. "Even though it happens very fast, you slow it down in your mind."

I glared at her. She was just repeating exactly what Patrick had said. I didn't believe she *really* understood it. I'll bet in school Ashley is one of those kids who always has to write down precisely what the teacher says.

"Okay, okay," I said. "I'll speed up to slow down." I didn't know what in the world I meant by those words, but if it would get Ashley to shut up, I'd say anything.

Patrick looked at me approvingly.

10

I took off on a run for my roundoff. A roundoff is a cartwheel with a quarter turn, so you end up facing the direction from which you came. I landed on my knees.

"Sorry," I said to Patrick. "I guess I slowed down enough . . . more like grinding to a halt."

"It was okay," said Patrick. "Even though you messed up, I could tell you were concentrating. That's what I want to see. I'm glad you understood what you did wrong."

"But I loused it up," I said, picking myself up.

"Don't worry," said Patrick. "Sometimes we have to take a move apart before we can put it together again."

I shook my head. None of what Patrick was saying made sense to me. I went back to stand in line.

It was Ashley's turn. "I'm going to slow down to speed up," she shouted to Patrick.

"Little parakeet," I mumbled.

"Maybe you should suggest a parrot for Ashley's Halloween costume," said Cindi. "When are we going to find out if Patrick's going to let us have that party?"

"I don't know," I said. "Nobody's said anything about it for two days. I figured you all thought the idea was stupid."

"No way," said Lauren. "I think it's a great idea."

11

"Then why didn't you nudge Patrick about it?" I asked.

"We were waiting for you," said Lauren.

"Patrick said he'd let us know," I said.

"Yeah, but you've got to ask him again," said Darlene. "He might have forgotten about it. I really want to do it."

"Then *you* ask him," I said.

Darlene shook her head. "It was your idea. I think you should ask him."

This was silly. We were making a big deal out of something so petty.

"Hey, Patrick!" I yelled. "Have you made up your mind about the Halloween party?"

Ashley finished her roundoff back-handspring. She put her hands on her hips and pouted. "Patrick, you weren't watching. I did it the best, and you weren't watching."

Patrick scratched his head. "I was hoping, since you hadn't mentioned it again, that you all had forgotten about the Halloween party," he said.

Mom looked up from across the room where she was working with a group of younger gymnasts. "What's this about a Halloween party?" she asked.

"Remember the great all-night Halloween parties we used to have in St. Louis?" I yelled. "The other day I told Patrick we should have one. Don't you think it's a neat idea?"

Patrick waved for Mom to take a break and come talk to him. "Let me hear about this event from an adult," he said.

Mom walked over to Patrick. "It was a lot of fun," she admitted.

"It sounds like a lot of work," said Patrick. "That's why I couldn't make up my mind. I'm kind of swamped right now."

Cindi nudged me. "He's going to say no," she whispered. "Do something."

"Why me?" I whispered back.

"Quick," said Lauren. "I know grown-ups. If they say no now, we won't get another chance."

"Uh . . . come on, Mom," I stammered. "It can't be so much work. You said yourself it's fun."

"Well, you have to get permission from all the parents, then you have to order the food, plan the games . . . it takes a lot of organizing."

"Great, Mom!" I said cheerfully. "You can show Patrick how to do it. You did it before."

"Whoa, Jodi," said Mom, shaking her head at me. "I'm scheduled to judge a gymnastics meet in Santa Fe on October thirtieth. Your aunt is coming to stay with you."

I had forgotten. I like my Aunt Robie. She's a lot of fun, and it isn't a tragedy spending a weekend with her. Still, I decided to milk it for all it was worth.

"Patrick, I'll be all alone," I pretended to sniff,

"an orphan on Halloween night." Mom started to laugh. She rubbed the top of my head with her knuckles.

"It sounds like a TV movie," said Darlene. "*An Orphan on Halloween Night*. Please, sir, can't she just come into the gym to warm up? And pleeeze, sir, we're just her friends. Can't we come in, too?"

Patrick started to chuckle. I knew I had him if I could make him laugh.

"We'll do all the work," I said quickly.

"All right, all right," said Patrick, throwing his hands in the air. "Your mom won't be able to chaperon, but I'll get my sister to help me out. She's at the University of Colorado, and she loves Halloween. You can have the Halloween party, but Jodi, you're in charge."

"Me?" I exclaimed.

"Your mom will tell you what to do. But you and the Pinecones will have to do all the work."

"I can't do that," I protested. "I can't organize my way out of a paper bag."

But Patrick didn't hear me protest. He couldn't because all the Pinecones had surrounded me and were clapping me on the back, congratulating me. I was a little worried. Being in charge was nothing I was used to.

Don't Worry
Be Happy

After practice I sat cross-legged on a bench in the locker room with my notebook in my hand. I started to make a list of what needed to be done for the party.

Becky came in and jiggled my knee with her leg. Apparently I was sitting in front of her locker. "Excuse me," she said in that wonderful snooty voice that makes me want to wipe the floor with her.

"Wait a minute," I said. "I want to finish what I'm doing."

"What's this? Jodi studying? Did some miracle happen that I didn't know about? Move, Jodi." Becky gave me a shove.

I ignored her and kept writing.

"She's slowed down to speed up," teased Ashley.

"If you must know, I'm making a list of everything we have to do for the party," I said, slowly rising and giving up my space to Becky. "Patrick put me in charge."

Becky started to laugh. "You've got to be kidding."

"What's so funny about me being in charge?" I asked.

"Yeah," said Lauren. "What's so funny?"

"Jodi's the biggest scatterbrain there is," exclaimed Becky. "All you Pinecones are lamebrained, but Jodi's the worst. She couldn't take charge of a paper bag."

Now, even though I had said the exact same thing myself, it made me furious to hear Becky say it. "I'd like to see your head in a paper bag," I snapped.

"It'd be an improvement," said Cindi. "Why don't you make a paper bag your costume, Becky?" Cindi smiled at Becky sweetly.

"Are you kidding? I wouldn't be seen dead at a party with you Pinecones. Your little Halloween in the gym sounds so joo-vi-nile."

"You're sooo wrong," I said. "It's going to be the best party ever. We're going to have the world's greatest haunted house because we can use all the equipment in the gym. We'll have great sound effects, a light show — it'll be a party that you'll never forget."

Becky put her hands on her hips. "And you're going to organize all this?"

"Yes, I am . . ." I said. I stood up on a bench. "I made a list," I announced. "The first thing we've got to do is write and mail out the permission slips. Tomorrow's Saturday. I think we should do it first thing in the morning."

"I can't," said Darlene. "I've got a dance lesson."

"I've got a piano lesson," said Lauren.

"We're going to visit my brother in college," said Cindi.

I glared at them.

"I could come," said Ti An. "But I can only write block letters. I can't write cursive yet."

"Great, great," I mumbled. "I'm supposed to do it all with a second-grader."

"Uh-oh," said Ti An.

"Now what?" I asked.

"I forgot. I've got a birthday party to go to tomorrow. I can't come."

Becky started laughing. "You're going to be a great organizer," she said. "I can just tell."

"You wouldn't think of helping out, would you?" I asked. Becky was an incredible pain in the neck, but she *was* smart and she was good at getting things done.

"Moi?" said Becky. "I wouldn't touch this party with a ten-foot pole. It's going to be a disaster."

"It is not," I said. "I still say it's going to be the best party ever."

"And I bet you can't pull it off," said Becky.

"Bet I can," I said, sounding like a two-year-old. "What do you want to bet?"

Becky laughed at me. "The loser will have to go around with a paper bag on her head for a whole day. That'll show everybody just what a fool you are."

I licked my lips. Bets make me nervous. I've lost an awful lot of them. I may act cocky, but I hate to be humiliated. Sometimes I bet on some fact that I'm absolutely sure I know, like what year Mary Lou Retton won the gold, and it turns out I'm wrong.

"Give me a minute to think about it," I said. "I want to consult the Pinecones."

"Chicken," said Becky. "Cluck . . . cluck . . . cluck." Ashley giggled. I scowled at her.

"You're supposed to be a Pinecone."

"Ashley's only being realistic," said Becky. "This has nothing to do with loyalty."

I hated Becky for mocking me. I'm the first to admit that I can be a little scatterbrained, but Becky made me so mad.

"You're the one who's going to have to back down," sneered Becky.

I took a menacing step toward her.

Cindi grabbed my arm and pulled me into the corner. "What are you in a sweat for?" she asked. "You can win this bet."

"Not if you guys don't help," I said. "I'll be the one going around with a paper bag over my head."

"Take her on, Jodi," whispered Darlene. "No way are you going to lose that bet."

"Oh, yeah?" I whispered back. "Will you skip your dance lesson and help me out tomorrow?"

Darlene shrugged. "I can't, but I'll help with the other stuff. Don't worry."

"Like the song says, 'Don't worry, be happy,' " sang Lauren.

I grinned. With the Pinecones behind me, I figured I couldn't lose. I turned back to Becky. "You're on," I said. "We're going to put on the Halloween party of the century."

Becky picked up her gym bag. "See you in a paper bag, chump," she said as she sauntered out of the locker room.

4

Measurements for a Paper Bag

Dear Mom or Dad of a gymnast at the Evergreen Gymnatic Academy,

This Halloween your child has a chance to be at the party of the century. We will be having an all-night Halloween Monster Bash at the gym. Patrick will be there as the resident chaperon-monster. And his sister will be helping out.

Each gymnast should come in costume and bring a sleeping bag. If you don't let your kid come it will be sad trick, 'cause your kid will miss some treat.

Trick or treat,
Jodi Sutton

P.S. Please sign this permission slip and send it back to Patrick right away or the goblins will get you.

I wrote the letter on our computer at home. I had gotten the addresses of all the gymnasts from Mom.

It was Saturday morning, and Mom was taking an adult gymnastics class at the Y. I read the letter over to myself. I liked it. I thought signing it *"Trick or treat"* was a great touch.

I picked up the phone to call Lauren and read it to her. She's the brainiest of the Pinecones, and I thought I should get her take on it.

Lauren's mom picked up the phone. Lauren's mom is kind of intimidating. She's on the school board, and she's a big muckamuck in Denver politics. Lauren says that one day her mom is going to run for mayor. All I know is that Mrs. Baca always answers the phone as if she's already busy. She doesn't say hello, she says "Yes?" and it sounds as if you'd better not waste her time.

"Hi, Mrs. Baca. It's Jodi Sutton. Is Lauren there?" I said all in one breath.

I could hear someone playing an old Beatles song on the piano. It sounded awful.

"Lauren has a piano lesson now," said Mrs. Baca. "And then right afterward I'm taking her shopping for new shoes. Can I have her call you this afternoon?"

"Uh, never mind. This afternoon will be too late."

"What's too late?" asked Mrs. Baca.

I thought for a moment about reading my letter to Mrs. Baca. After all, she was on the school board, and she was a parent.

Then I got embarrassed. "Never mind," I said quickly. " 'Bye." I hung up.

I read my letter again. It sounded good to me. Mom had told me the most important thing was to get the letter out right away because there were less than two weeks before Halloween. She hadn't said to wait and let her read it. If nobody else was around to help, what was I supposed to do?

I printed out all the copies of the letter. Sometimes when I was tearing away the little holes from the computer paper, I ripped it, but this wasn't like a school project, where neatness counted. I stuck stamps on all the envelopes. Then I rode my bicycle down to the post office and put the letters in the box there so they'd get into the mail as soon as possible.

I felt terrific. Once the letters were in the mailbox, I didn't have to worry about them anymore. Writing the permission slip had seemed like such a big deal, and I had complained about having to do it myself, but it really hadn't been all that much work.

I rode back feeling very proud of myself. I had done the whole job entirely on my own. Becky would be wearing a paper bag on *her* head for a week!

On Monday when I went to gymnastics, Patrick was on the phone in his office on the second floor. He was standing in the doorway. He waved down at me. I waved back.

I went to the mats to warm up. Darlene was wearing her hair in a new style. The front was braided, and the back was loose.

"I like your hair," I said.

"That's good," said Darlene, " 'cause it cost a lot of money for the braids, and Mom says that even if I don't like it, I have to live with it until after Halloween. I figure it will go well with my cowgirl outfit."

"We learned in history about black cowboys," I said, "so I guess there must have been black cowgirls."

"There are on the Bronco cheerleading squad," said Darlene. "That's the kind of cowgirl I'm going as. What's your costume going to be?"

"I want to be a mummy," I said.

"That's not so unusual," said Ashley. "I mean,

your mommy wears jogging suits and leotards. How's anybody going to know what you are?"

"Not a mommy, dummy, a *mummy*," I said. "I've already got my costume figured out. I'm going to wrap bandages around my long underwear, then paint drops of blood on them. . . ."

"Yuk . . . " said Ashley. "That's scary."

"The whole point of Halloween is to be scary," I said. "What are you going as? A princess?"

Ashley smiled. "How did you guess? That's one of my first choices. I might go as a princess or a ballerina . . . a prom queen. . . ."

"A princess . . . a ballerina? How original!" mocked Lauren.

"You kids are obsessed with Halloween," said Becky. She did a perfect split.

I watched her. It made me so mad that Becky is both incredibly flexible and strong. Becky did a handstand and arched her back so that her feet were practically parallel to the floor. She looked beautiful.

"I wish I could do that," said Ashley.

"You will," said Becky. "All it takes is practice. Something the other Pinecones aren't too keen on doing. They'd rather talk about their costumes."

"We are, too, warming up," I said, as I did a handstand and tried to add the arch.

Suddenly I heard Patrick yell, "JODI!"

I fell over in a heap. "What's wrong?" I asked. "Was I arched too much?"

Patrick wasn't interested in my handstand. "What did you say in that letter of yours?" he asked. "I've been getting calls from parents all afternoon."

"What letter?" asked Becky. "I didn't get any letter."

"Your mother got it when you were in school," said Patrick. "She was one of the first people to call."

"You mean, people got them already? That's terrific," I said. "I rode all the way to the post office because I know the mail goes out faster from there."

I sat up expecting some kind of appreciation.

"I've been getting calls about a 'Monster Bash,' " said Patrick. "The parents sound confused. They want to know what we have in mind. What in the world did you write?"

Becky pantomimed putting a paper bag over her head. Then she spread her fingers over my head.

"What are you doing?" I asked her.

"I'm measuring your head for a paper bag," she said. Ashley giggled.

I wanted to drop-kick Becky across the gym, but first I had Patrick to deal with. He looked very mad. And Patrick's not like me. Patrick almost never loses his temper. I had a feeling I was in deep trouble.

5

No Way Out

"I have a copy of the letter in my knapsack," I said to Patrick.

"Go get it," he growled.

I jumped up, my face bright red. I brought the piece of paper to Patrick.

Patrick read it. "Didn't your mom check this before you sent it out?" he asked.

"She was at class," I said. "You said I was in charge. What's wrong with it? I put in that you would be chaperoning. Mom said that was important. It's supposed to be funny. It's not the pledge of allegiance."

"It is funny, Jodi," said Patrick without cracking a smile. "That's the problem."

"Read it to us," said Becky.

Darlene scrunched up next to me. "What did you write?" she whispered.

"Why didn't you let us hear it first?" Lauren whispered into my other ear.

"You were all busy," I said, pouting.

Patrick read my letter to himself again. I thought I saw the corners of his mouth turn up, but I wasn't sure. "I think some parents misinterpreted it," he said.

"Read it out loud," Becky demanded again.

Patrick looked at me. "Do you mind?" he asked.

I shrugged. "Everybody will see it anyway. I mailed it to everyone."

Patrick started to read aloud. When he got to the part about, "the party of the century . . . an all-night Halloween Monster Bash at the gym," Lauren started giggling. Darlene laughed out loud when Patrick read, "if you don't let your kid come, it will be sad trick, 'cause your kid will miss some treat."

"I signed it 'Trick or treat', too," I said. I liked it that everybody was chuckling. It made me feel good that I could make people laugh with something I wrote.

Patrick shook his head. "A few parents thought we were going to have a punk rock party in our gym."

"Let me see it, will you?" Becky asked Patrick.

Patrick handed Becky the note. "Jodi can't even spell gymnastics," she said. "Jodi spelled it g-y-m-n-a-t-i-c. It sounds like a foreign car."

"Very funny," I mumbled.

"And look," said Becky's friend Gloria. "Jodi couldn't even spell permission right. She left out an s."

"I didn't know I was going to be graded on spelling."

"You wrote it on a computer," said Becky. "Were you too lazy to use the spelling checker?"

I glared at her. Nothing hurts as much as when someone you hate is right. I *had* been too lazy to check the spelling.

"It's got a few spelling mistakes," said Patrick with a smile, "but it's not as bad as I expected. All right, enough about this party. I'll call the parents and tell them what to expect. It's not your fault, Jodi. I shouldn't have put it all on you."

I knew Patrick was trying to make me feel better, but he was making it worse.

"I knew you'd screw it up," said Becky.

"She didn't screw it up," said Cindi defensively. We heard the phone ring in Patrick's office.

"It's probably another parent, calling to complain," said Becky.

Patrick gave me back my letter. "I'm sorry," I

said. He went to answer the phone. I followed him. I felt I owed him a private apology.

I heard Patrick explain to yet another parent that, no, there would not be a live rock band at the party, no the party was not open to teenagers, except those girls who were gymnasts and yes, he and his sister would be there all night as chaperons.

Patrick hung up the phone and scratched his head. "Well, you've certainly stirred everybody up with your party," he said. "I hope it's worth it."

"Becky was right. I really did screw it up."

Patrick rubbed the back of his neck. "Well, it would have been nice if you had shown the letter to your mom or me before you sent it out, but it's a great letter. It might not be appropriate, but it's a great letter."

"Are you going to call off the party?" I asked Patrick.

"No way. I'm getting psyched for it. I'll simply explain to the parents that I'll be here all night, and there is nothing to worry about. I'm still counting on you to plan all the games and whatever else you want to do."

I thought about it. If I had messed up a simple little letter, think of how I could screw up the whole party. I didn't want to do it. "I think you'd better give this job to somebody else," I said.

"Hold on there, Jodi. This was your idea. You're not backing out."

"But I'm not the type to be responsible." At least I was being honest. I thought Patrick would be proud of me for being honest.

"How will you ever learn if you don't try?" said Patrick. I hate it when adults say something like that to you. It gives you no way out.

"I *am* sorry," I said again.

"Forget it," said Patrick. "You can make it up to me by working doubly hard on gymnastics today."

"Gymnastics!" I exclaimed. "How can I think of gymnastics when I have a Halloween party to plan?"

"Come on," said Patrick. "There's more to life than worrying about parties. Let's go."

We walked out to the gym together.

6

So Mad
I Could Spit

"Listen up," said Patrick when we sat down on the crash mats. "We've spent enough time on Halloween. I want to practice some dance moves. I've been noticing lately that all your dance moves have gotten very sloppy."

Patrick stood at the edge of the mats. He did a series of stride leaps across the floor. Then he did cat leaps coming back. He really looked like a cat. "What did you hear when I landed?" he asked.

We all looked at each other. "Nothing," I muttered.

"Exactly, Jodi," said Patrick. "Very good."

I beamed. It wasn't often that I came up with the right answer.

"The only thing Jodi's good for is nothing," said Becky. "Now, if only we didn't have to hear her."

"Becky," warned Patrick. "That's enough. You heard almost nothing when I landed, and that's what I want to hear when *you* land." Patrick did a cat leap again.

"You look like a ballet dancer," said Lauren.

"Thank you. Line up, everybody. I want to see you do split leaps across the mat. Then I want you to come back doing cat leaps. Ti An, you're first."

Ti An is a wonderful dancer. She almost floated across the floor.

Lauren was next. "It's a proven fact that dancers are born, not made," she said as she started down the mats. Lauren was not nearly as graceful as Ti An. "Point those hoofs, point those hoofs," Patrick yelled at her when she was halfway across.

Lauren looked back and giggled.

"Okay, Jodi. Your turn," said Patrick. I'm a terrible dancer. I love tumbling, but I always lose points on the dance parts of my floor routines.

I got my left and right arm mixed up. One arm is supposed to go up when you leap, but I always forget which one.

"Jodi!" shouted Patrick. "What are you doing?"

"A cat leap."

"It sounded more like a monkey leaping," said Patrick. I heard Becky guffaw across the gym.

"Maybe Jodi's coming as a monkey for Halloween," she said. "That would be appropriate."

Ashley giggled.

"I know where you can rent a monkey costume," shouted Becky.

"I already have my costume," I yelled back.

"Jodi, cut it out," said Patrick.

"What did I do?" I complained. "I just said I had my costume. I'm coming as a mummy. And I'll bring extra bandages so that I can wrap a few around Becky's mouth."

"I'd like to gag both of you for a little while," said Patrick. "It would give us all a little peace. Next." Cindi leaped down the mats. She always gets this look of incredible concentration on her face, but she wasn't very good, either. "Point those flippers, point those flippers!" yelled Patrick.

Cindi looked back at him. "Which is it? Flippers or hoofs?" she asked seriously.

"I'm not looking for a circus act. I want to see pointed toes," said Patrick.

"Maybe we should go as a menagerie for Halloween," I said after I finished. I sat on the bench to catch my breath.

"Just go as yourselves, the Pinecone Klutzes," said Becky. She laughed.

"Very funny, motor mouth."

"Jodi," whispered Cindi.

"What's wrong?" I whispered back.

"Stop goading Becky. It'll only get you into trouble. Don't let her teasing get to you."

"She doesn't bother me," I lied.

But Becky refused to let me alone. "Jodi," she taunted, "you don't need a costume because I've already got yours. A great big garbage bag."

"Who are you calling garbage?" I said, grabbing her by the arm.

"Jodi!" yelled Patrick from across the floor. "You and Becky stay out of each other's way. I've had it up to here with this sniping. One more argument and you'll both be in trouble with me."

"See you around," said Becky. "See you in a paper bag."

I started after her. Darlene grabbed me. "Jodi, watch it. Cool down."

"She makes me so mad," I answered.

"I know," said Darlene. "But didn't you hear what Patrick said? You're going to be in big trouble if you keep this up."

"Becky started it," I said.

Darlene just looked at me. I sighed. I sounded like a two-year-old. But I couldn't help myself.

Becky made me so mad I could spit.

I watched as Becky demonstrated a perfect series of split leaps down the mat. If only she weren't so good — *that* was the problem. If it ever came to having to choose between Becky or me, I knew who Patrick would pick. Becky was the better gymnast, hands down.

7

The Becky Problem

I put a list up in the locker room asking for volunteers to help plan the party the weekend before Halloween.

Lauren was the first to sign up. "You didn't put down what time," she said.

"I was afraid," I admitted. "I figured any time I picked, somebody would have something else planned."

"But you have to pick a time," said Lauren. "Otherwise you'll be changing it every minute."

"Well, are you willing to help?" I asked.

"Of course," said Lauren. "That's why I'm standing here with my pencil in my hand."

"No piano lessons?" I asked sarcastically.

"I can do it after my piano lesson," she said.

"Can we do it at two o'clock on Saturday?"

"Okay, we'll make it two o'clock Saturday," I said.

"What's two o'clock Saturday?" asked Darlene, coming into the locker room. She was wearing tiger-patterned leg warmers.

"Is that part of a costume?" I asked.

Darlene shook her head. "It's my latest fashion statement. So, what's at two o'clock?" she asked.

"The meeting to plan the games for Halloween," I said.

"Can we do it at three?" asked Darlene. "I'm supposed to pick up my cowgirl costume at Mile High Stadium at one o'clock, and it'll be easier if we do it at three."

"Fine. Three o'clock," I said.

"Wait a minute," said Cindi. "I want to help. But Cleo has to go to the vet, and I'm supposed to take her."

"Can't you get somebody else to take her?" I asked, thoroughly exasperated. "This is crazy. We'll never find a time that we all can do it."

"I guess so," said Cindi.

I went over to my list and put down *THREE O'CLOCK* in big letters. "There," I said. "That's final."

Ti An came in and looked at the piece of paper. "I know, I know," I said. "You want to help, but you can't do it until four. You're going to ask me if we can change the meeting to four P.M."

Ti An turned to face me, her pencil in her hand. "No, I can come," she said. "It's just that you put it up so high I can't reach it."

I giggled. I was beginning to take myself just a little bit too seriously. I took the paper down, but when I went to stick it lower on the wall, it wouldn't stay. Ti An tried pressing the tape with her thumb, but the minute she took her thumb away, the paper floated to the ground.

"What's going on in here?" asked Becky, coming into the locker room to change and seeing Ti An leaning against the wall. "Let me guess. You goons are going to play pin-the-tail-on-the-donkey for your Halloween party, and Ti An's the donkey."

"I am not," said Ti An. "This is Jodi's sign-up sheet to work for the party and I'm holding it."

Becky rolled her eyes toward the ceiling. "That's Jodi. She needs three people to help her put up a notice. Ever wondered how many Pinecones it takes to screw in a light bulb?"

"How many?" I asked, knowing that I shouldn't.

"None. It's easier to burn the Pinecones than use a light bulb," said Becky.

Gloria laughed, but I thought Becky's joke was incredibly mean.

"Becky, were you born a witch or did something make you this way?" I asked her.

"You're the one who's got Halloween on the brain. I have better things to do, like gymnastics."

Becky went over to her locker. Darlene shook her head at me. "*Now* what did I do wrong?" I protested.

"You're letting her get you every time," she said. "Ignore her. That will really drive Becky crazy. She just loves it that she can get you riled."

"It's because Jodi's Irish," said Cindi. "Hot temper."

"Hey, guys," pleaded Ti An. "Do I have to hold this all day?"

"Just a second," I said. "I'll get some tape from Patrick." I ran out of the locker room and up to Patrick's office. He was sitting at his desk with his feet up, talking on the phone.

He motioned for me to come in as he put the receiver back into its cradle.

"Another parent mad about my note?" I asked.

Patrick shook his head. "Believe it or not, there are more things going on in the world than the Halloween party. That was Coach Darrell Miller."

"The coach of the Atomic Amazons?" I asked. The Atomic Amazons are a club in Denver that almost always beats us in competition.

"We're setting up some meets for the winter." Patrick rubbed his hand through his hair.

"Maybe after Halloween, you and the Pinecones will get the cobwebs out of your brains and begin concentrating on gymnastics again."

"It's just until next weekend," I said. "I'm sorry."

"You don't have to be sorry, Jodi," said Patrick. "I think it's terrific that you're doing all this work for your friends."

"Becky doesn't think so," I said.

Patrick frowned. "I didn't mention Becky. Why, when I compliment you, do you have to bring up your rivalry with Becky?"

I shrugged.

"Jodi, I meant what I said on the floor the other day. I may have to get a court order for both you and Becky to cease and desist."

"What does that mean?" I asked.

"It means I don't like the way you two constantly goad each other."

"But she makes me so mad," I complained. "She's always criticizing me."

"You worry about your own temper, and let me worry about Becky," said Patrick sternly. "Now, what did you want? I *hope* it wasn't to come in here and complain about Becky."

I shook my head quickly. "I just needed a piece of tape," I said.

Patrick handed me the dispenser. "Don't tell me. It's got something to do with Halloween? Are

41

you getting all the help you need?"

"Ti An's holding up her end," I said as I hurried out of Patrick's office to relieve Ti An.

She was still waiting for me. The other girls had gone out into the gym to warm up.

"Are you getting tired?" I asked. "You could have just left it."

"I didn't want to let you down," said Ti An. "Besides, I was worried that Becky might do something to it if I just left it. Why is Becky so mean?"

"Don't worry about Becky," I said to Ti An. "She's my problem, not yours."

Then I realized that those were almost the same words Patrick had said to me. If you asked me, Becky was just one big problem that constantly got passed around.

Tumbling Well Is the Best Revenge

Patrick had us working on our tumbling again, the old roundoff back-handspring. I tried to concentrate on what he had told me the last time, to slow down to speed up.

"Slow it down," I mumbled to myself as I took my run.

Patrick stopped me even before I could begin my roundoff. "Jodi, what are you looking for?" he asked.

I stopped short. "Huh?" I felt like an idiot.

"You're looking at the ground as you run. Are you looking for pennies?"

Becky giggled. "She's looking for her feet, so she won't trip on them."

"Becky," warned Patrick. He turned back to

me. "Jodi, keep your head up when you start your tumbling run. After all, you're going up in the air. You're not digging for gold."

I heard Ashley and Becky laugh behind me.

"I guess I was looking down because I was concentrating on slowing down," I said.

"The place to think about slowing down is right after the roundoff, but it's not exactly slowing down . . . in real time, I want you to go as fast as ever. It's your internal clock I'm talking about. Do you understand? But as you start, you have to think about going up."

"I don't think Jodi can keep two things in her mind at the same time," said Becky.

I glared at her.

"Becky, button up," said Patrick. "Keep your responses to yourself."

"In other words, shut up," I said.

"Jodi," warned Patrick. "I'll deal with Becky. Did you understand what I was saying about your 'internal clock'?" he asked. I nodded my head yes. It seemed easier than telling Patrick that he was talking gobbledygook as far as I was concerned.

Patrick looked me in the eye. "Are you 'yessing' me or do you understand?"

"Yessing you," I admitted.

Patrick put his hand on my shoulder. "Well, at

least you're honest. Forget about it for a little while. It will seep in slowly."

"I don't know, Patrick," Becky said. "Jodi's got a pretty thick skull."

"Becky," snapped Patrick. "I warned you. Remember what we spoke about earlier? Mind your own business."

"Right, nosy-nose," I taunted, glad that Patrick was mad at her.

"And you, Jodi Sutton. . . . I've told you both. This sniping has got to stop."

I went to the end of the line. "Becky makes me so mad," I muttered to Lauren who was the last in line.

"Yeah, me, too," said Lauren. "But she's making scrambled eggs out of your head. Forget about her."

"That's what everybody says," I mumbled. "I just wish I could think of some way to shut her up for good."

"My mom always says that living well is the best revenge. Maybe tumbling well is the best revenge," said Lauren.

"Is that a proven fact?" I teased. Lauren loves to come up with proven facts.

"I don't know," said Lauren. "But it's a proven fact that even I'm getting tired of you and Becky fighting all the time. You've got to control that

Irish temper of yours at least until she's out of our hair."

"Just 'cause I'm Irish, everybody always thinks I've got a temper. That makes me mad."

Lauren laughed at me. I could feel myself getting seriously mad at Lauren. What right did she have to tell me to control my temper? It was all Becky's fault.

We moved up in line. Lauren went next. Her legs were bent, and she was a little sloppy, but Lauren's got this natural explosiveness. She always gets great height. I watched her closely.

When she finished she turned back and grinned at me. I gave her a thumbs-up sign. I couldn't be mad at Lauren very long.

Patrick nodded to me. I took off. I concentrated on keeping my head up. I got a lot of height on my roundoff, and as I landed I actually had a moment to think about my jump for the handspring. I don't know if I actually did slow down to speed up, but it was the best roundoff back-handspring I had ever done.

"All right!" said Patrick. I saw out of the corner of my eye that Becky had been watching me. She looked very disgruntled.

I got back in line again. "Maybe you're right," I admitted to Lauren. "Maybe tumbling well is the best revenge."

9

Midnight . . .
The Witching Hour

The next day I looked up on the wall to see how many people had signed up to work with me on the games. I saw all right. I saw red.

Someone had taken a thick black pen and crossed out *THREE O'CLOCK*. Instead they had written *MIDNIGHT, THE WITCHING HOUR*. It was scribbled all over my announcement so that I couldn't read the names underneath.

I gathered all the Pinecones and made them come see. "Look!" I complained. I pointed to my announcement.

Lauren started to giggle.

"What's so funny?" I demanded.

"*Midnight . . . the witching hour*," sang Lauren in a half-spooky voice. "The hour for planning weird games." She cackled like a witch.

"How can you think it's funny?" I asked. "It's defacing my announcement!"

" 'Defacing your announcement!' " teased Lauren. "You sound like my mother. She always says 'Defacing public property is a disgrace.' It's one of her favorite sayings. She thinks it rhymes."

"Well, I think this is a disgrace," I said.

Lauren squinted at the announcement. "It's just us Pinecones who have signed up to help with the haunted house. What's the big deal? We'll all still be there."

"It's the principle of the thing. I know who did this," I said.

"Becky," said Darlene, Jodi, Lauren, Ti An, and Ashley together.

"Are you guys making fun of me?" I asked.

"You're getting a little hysterical," said Cindi. "Come on, Jodi. If this were Becky's announcement, you'd be the first one to think it was funny to write something stupid on it."

"Thank you all very much," I snapped.

I heard someone laughing behind me. I twirled around. Becky had walked into the locker room. She put her gym bag down on the bench with a bang.

"Well, well, if it isn't the little coven of witches, having a meeting."

"Don't even bother to deny it," I said.

Becky just laughed at me. "Deny what, little witch?"

"You wrote on my announcement," I said. "You're just trying to win your bet by cheating."

I leaped over a bench and lunged for Becky. Darlene tried to grab me but I slipped out of her hands.

Becky took a backwards step. "Temper, temper, Jodi podi," she taunted me.

I wanted to take a swing at her.

"You've been trying to sabotage my Halloween party ever since I started planning it," I yelled at her. "That's all you want to do." I was so mad at Becky that I tore my announcement from the wall, wadded it into a ball, and threw it at her. It glanced off her arm.

"I'm going to tell Patrick you are out of control," yelled Becky.

"Tattletale," I snarled at her.

"Little creep," snapped Becky.

Becky grabbed her gymnastics slippers and ran out of the locker room. I went to follow her, but Darlene grabbed me.

"Jodi! You'll get yourself kicked out of gymnastics for fighting," said Darlene.

"Let me at her. I don't care. I want to wallop her."

"You can't," said Cindi.

"I can, too. I don't care how strong she is."

49

"Who cares about how strong she is? She's going to get you in trouble!" yelled Lauren.

I took a deep breath. My friends were right.

Suddenly there was a loud thumping noise on the door to the locker room.

Patrick's voice came through loud and clear. "What is going on in there?" He pounded on the door again. "Jodi, I want to see you in my office before class as soon as you're changed."

"*Now* you've done it," warned Cindi. "Becky probably ran straight to Patrick. I bet he's going to call off your Halloween party."

"If he does, it's all Becky's fault," I said.

Ti An sat on the bench. "Are you in trouble?" she asked me. She looked worried.

"Naw. Becky's the one who's in trouble," I said. "I'm sure Patrick understands that she always starts it."

"That's not strictly true," said Darlene.

"Hey, you guys, it's Becky we're talking about here. How can you believe it's *my* fault? She just wants to ruin the Halloween party so she can win the bet."

"And you're the sap," said Lauren. "You fall for it every time."

Darlene nodded her head. "Lauren's right. You're like Silly Putty. You play right into Becky's hands."

"What are you talking about?" I was getting very steamed.

"Every time you lose your temper, you just prove Becky's right. If you go into Patrick's office and tattle, you'll be the one who's in trouble. Patrick hates it when we tattle on each other."

"I wish we could all go with Jodi," said Lauren.

"I could use a few bodyguards against Becky."

"We were thinking more along the lines of protecting you from yourself," said Lauren.

"Maybe we should muzzle Jodi before she goes to see Patrick," said Darlene. She didn't sound as if she were kidding.

"I'll be fine," I protested. "I don't know why you're so worried."

Darlene grabbed my arm. "Keep cool," she said. "Don't blow it."

I shook loose. "Why don't you worry about Becky instead of me?" I demanded.

"Because Becky always keeps her cool," said Darlene. "It's your temper that I'm worried about."

10

A Fishy Handshake

Patrick was nervously tapping a pencil on his desk when I walked in. Becky was sitting on the edge of one of the folding chairs. She was leaning over his desk, talking very low.

She stopped talking when I entered the room. I knew she was telling Patrick it was all my fault.

"Jodi," said Patrick, "please sit down."

"I didn't do anything," I said, as I sat opposite Becky.

"Becky tells me you threw something at her," said Patrick.

I could feel myself turning red. I squirmed in

my seat and twisted my legs up onto the chair. "I didn't really."

Patrick frowned at me. "What does 'really' mean?" he asked.

"I didn't throw anything hard at her," I said. "I couldn't have hurt her."

"It's the principle of the thing," said Becky.

"It was a lousy piece of paper," I yelled. I was about to burst, I was so mad.

"She could have blinded me," protested Becky.

"Girls," said Patrick. His voice wasn't loud, but he sounded so disgusted and angry that both of us shut up. "I've had enough. I've warned you both separately that I don't like the way you talk to each other. I certainly will not tolerate physical abuse."

I guffawed at the words "physical abuse."

Patrick frowned at me. "Jodi, for once Becky is right. It is the principle of the thing. You had no right to throw *anything* at Becky."

"It's behavior inappropriate to a gymnast," said Becky. "But it's about what you'd expect from a Pinecone."

"Becky, button your lip," said Patrick. "I'll decide what's appropriate for a gymnast."

"See, Patrick?" I said. "Becky always has to have the last word, and the first word. She's the one who should be ashamed. She's the one who tattled."

"I am ashamed of both of you," thundered Patrick. "I called you in here because I want an end to this. You're going to force me to do something I don't want to do. I'd like you both to come up with some constructive suggestions about how you can learn to work together."

"Well, for one thing, Jodi could learn to respect gymnastics," said Becky.

I stared at her. "What does that mean?"

"You come from this great gymnastics family, and you're always goofing off."

"First of all, I don't always goof off," I argued. "And second of all, what does my family have to do with you?"

"It just tees me off, that's all," said Becky. "It's like you should have been born with talent, instead of no-talent. If I were born into your family, I'd be in the Olympics."

"Jodi's an individual, Becky," said Patrick. "She's not just an extension of her family. You've got to respect Jodi as an individual."

"Yeah," I said. I untwisted my legs and leaned forward. "That's the whole problem in a nutshell," I said to Patrick. "Becky doesn't respect my individuality. If she did that, there'd be no problem."

"Bull," said Becky. "Jodi flies off the handle every time I look at her."

"Is that true, Jodi?" Patrick asked me.

"Becky never gives me *anything* except dirty looks," I said.

"Give me a break," said Becky with a sigh. "Jodi's so wrapped up in her stupid Halloween party, that's all she cares about. She doesn't give a fig for gymnastics. She's a bad example. The Pinecones are a sorry enough group to be associated with the Evergreen Academy. But ever since Jodi got that stupid idea for her Halloween party, that's all they care about."

I waited for Becky to tell Patrick the truth, that she had made a bet with me that I would make a mess of the party and now she was doing all she could to see that it was fouled up for sure.

But Becky kept quiet.

I bit my lip. I wasn't going to be a tattletale and tell on her. That wasn't my style. I did mutter, "I think the party's going to be great, no matter what you do to spoil it."

"Bet it won't," said Becky under her breath.

"Girls," snapped Patrick. "None of this is constructive. You're making it worse. Becky, you're a creative person. Can you come up with a solution?"

"Yeah. Put me in charge of the party. That way you'll have a success."

Patrick shook his head. "Absolutely not. The party was Jodi's idea. It's her baby."

Becky stood up. "Then whatever happens will be on Jodi's head."

"Is that a threat?" I said, half getting up out of my seat.

"Becky, Jodi," snapped Patrick. "I have had it up to here with this sniping. I had hoped, Becky, that working with the Pinecones might mellow you. It seems to have had the reverse effect."

"That's Becky, always going in reverse," I said.

"And, Jodi, I had hoped you would learn something about dedication and hard work from Becky. I want you to both shake hands now and promise me you will stop it. You don't have to be best friends. But you are both gymnasts with the Evergreen Academy and you have to at least respect each other and leave each other alone."

"I've got the solution," said Becky. "I won't show up. It's way too joo-ve-nile. You can have the party without me. I think it's just for babies anyhow. I don't want to be seen with Pinecones any more than necessary."

"Do you mean that?" I asked. The idea of having the party without Becky was heavenly. "What about our bet?" I said suspiciously.

Becky shrugged. "I can find out how it went.

You'll still be wearing a paper bag."

"What is this about a bet?" Patrick asked.

"Nothing," Becky and I said in unison. I think it's the first thing we ever agreed upon.

"Becky," said Patrick, "I want you to solemnly promise that you will do nothing to sabotage Jodi's Halloween party."

I liked the sound of that: "Jodi's Halloween party." I grinned.

Patrick was not smiling. "Jodi, I want you to promise that you will keep your temper, no matter how much you're provoked. I want the two of you to shake hands."

I stood up warily and extended my hand. It hung out in the air. Becky looked at my hand as if it were a smelly flounder that she was going to have to touch.

She shook the ends of my fingers. It was a creepy handshake, but it seemed to satisfy Patrick.

"All right," he said. "If you can't learn to get along, I will have to take drastic measures."

Becky and I looked at each other. Patrick didn't have to spell out the drastic measures. We both understood he meant that the gym wasn't big enough for both of us.

"Now I don't want to hear any more stories of the two of you flying off the handle at each other," warned Patrick.

"I'm not the one with a temper," said Becky.

"Becky!" warned Patrick.

"Sorry," said Becky. "Can I go now? I'd rather practice gymnastics than worry about this junk."

"It's not junk. Getting along, even with people you don't like, is as much a part of gymnastics as learning a new trick," said Patrick. "However, let's all go back to gymnastics."

Becky flounced out of Patrick's office.

"Do you think she means it?" I asked Patrick.

"Means what?" asked Patrick.

"Means that maybe she won't go to the party."

Patrick almost exploded. "Jodi, did you listen to anything I said just now?"

I nodded.

"You don't want me and Becky to fight anymore."

"I want you to make an extra effort to get along with Becky." Patrick rubbed his neck. He sighed. "Jodi, promise me one thing."

"What's that?" I asked.

"No more party crises, please. Don't make me regret that I ever said yes."

"You won't," I promised Patrick. But I wasn't absolutely sure I could keep that promise. It all depended on Becky.

11

I Don't Want
Your Stupid Jack

Mom came into my room just as I was putting the finishing touches on my list for the meeting about the Halloween games. Since I had started planning the party, it seemed all I was doing was making lists.

My bedroom isn't very big. Mom had to step over what looked like a pile of dirty clothes to get to my bed. "Jodi, what is this mess? Do you want me to take it down to the laundry?"

"Don't touch that!" I yelped. "It's my mummy costume. I still have a little work to do on it. I sewed bandages on my long johns. It's neat."

"You'll have to try it on for me before I go tomorrow," said Mom. "What can I do to help?"

I looked up from my list. "How much does spaghetti cost?" I asked.

"Not very much," said Mom. "Is that what you're planning on living on while I'm away?"

"No," I said. "I need tons of it for guts. We'll blindfold each gymnast and make them walk the beam. Then they'll jump off the beam into a pile of slimy spaghetti, and we'll tell them it's the guts of all the gymnasts who went before. Won't that be great?"

Mom looked a little doubtful.

"It's going to be better than anything we ever did in St. Louis. My committee is coming to help me plan it. But I want to have some surprises even for the committee. This is my show."

Mom nodded. "Patrick and I were talking about how proud we are of you for the way you've taken charge."

I looked up at Mom warily. I know my mother. Whenever she has something bad to tell me she always tries to start out with something positive. When she told me that she and Dad were getting divorced, she started out by saying she thought I'd love learning how to ski. That's how I found out Mom and I were moving to Denver.

The fact that she likes to emphasize the positive makes her a great coach — for other gymnasts, but not for me. She's my mom, and I know her too well. Sometimes I tease her about it.

When she used to try to coach me in gymnastics, she'd search so hard for something good to say that it was ridiculous. I used to get queasy just doing a backward roll. Mom would compliment me for not throwing up on the mats.

"Okay, Mom," I said. "What have I been doing wrong?"

Mom looked up, a little startled. "I just told you about all the things you're doing right. I think the party's going to be a terrific success. Patrick told me that more than twenty kids have signed up to come."

"Uh-huh," I said. I put down my list. "And. . . ."

"And, I want to talk to you about Becky," said Mom.

I slammed my notebook down on my bed. I was really angry. "I already talked to Patrick about Becky. Did he ask you to talk to me, too? That stinks. I *hate* that you work with Patrick. Don't you and Patrick have something better to do than gossip about how mad . . ?" I paused. I had meant to say how "bad" I was, but it came out how "mad." I stopped talking and took a breath. "It's unfair. None of the other Pinecones have to have their moms knowing every little thing that goes on."

"Watch your temper, Jodi. Don't jump to conclusions. Patrick didn't talk to me about anything. I've been listening to Becky. Remember,

I'm helping Becky in her rehabilitation."

"I'd like to rehabilitate her into outer space."

"Well, she's almost ready to go back to the elite group," said Mom. "You and she are always mouthing off about each other. It's getting out of hand."

"Why are you mad at me because Becky's such a witch? It's not *my* fault."

"I'm not mad at you," said Mom. "That's where you jumped the gun. Have you ever heard the story about the man who gets a flat tire?"

I shook my head. "Is this going to be one of those stories I'm supposed to learn from?" I asked.

Mom smiled. "Yes. Anyhow, a man gets a flat tire on a deserted country road, and he sees a farmhouse in the distance. He decides to walk to the farmhouse to ask for a jack. But as he's walking, he starts thinking, I'll bet the farmer hates strangers. I'll bet the farmer isn't going to help me. I'll bet the farmer slams the door in my face.

"He finally gets to the farmhouse, and the farmer innocently opens the door. The man yells at him, 'I don't want your stupid jack!' "

Sometimes Mom's stories are pretty stupid. "What does that have to do with me?"

"Sometimes you think you know what people are going to say to you, and you get mad right away, even before anyone does anything to you."

"That's got nothing to do with Becky. She *does* hate me, and she never fails to do something to make me mad. It's not like the farmer at all," I protested.

"Well, maybe," said Mom. "But you're letting your feelings about Becky drift into other parts of your life. Becky isn't worth it. You're going to meet all kinds of people in your life that you don't like. You've got to learn to live with them and get on with what's important to you."

"That's sort of what Patrick said, too," I said. "But I can't just ignore Becky and let her bully me."

"Maybe ignoring her would be the best revenge," said Mom.

"Lauren says that doing well in gymnastics is the best revenge. But I'll never be as good as Becky."

"Oh, boy, are you wrong!" said Mom.

I looked up at her, surprised. "Come off it, Mom. You know Becky's better than I am. She always will be."

"She may be a better gymnast," said Mom. "But she'll never be a better person than you are."

"Thanks," I said sarcastically. "It's easy for you to say," I said. "You're my mother."

"Do me a favor," said Mom.

"What's that?" I never like to promise Mom a

favor unless I know exactly what it is.

"Just enjoy your Halloween party. Don't let Becky ruin it."

"I won't . . . if she stays out of my way," I said. "She's promised not to come. That's the only way it'll be a success. If you guarantee she won't show up, I'll have a good time."

Mom sighed. "That's not good enough, Jodi, and you know it."

I knew what Mom wanted. I knew what Patrick wanted. But I didn't know what Becky was planning. I knew one thing. I wasn't just going to wimp out and let Becky get away with ruining my party. No way would I let her do that.

12

An Almost
Fatal Error

I had ordered the spaghetti, my special noise-makers, and the sponges (for dripping fake blood). Everything was ready, including my mummy costume.

The day before the party, the Pinecones had come over to my house to help with the final countdown. I was psyched. I had planned plenty of surprises, even for the Pinecones.

"I've got my costume all ready," said Lauren. "I'm going as a hot dog. Mom made me a bun out of yellow foam rubber, and I'm wearing a red leotard that I painted mustard on."

"I'm going as a ballerina," said Cindi. "I got this great tutu at a garage sale last week. It's pink. My brother says I look like a fruitcake, but I love it. It's got sequins."

"My cowgirl cheerleader costume has sequins, too," said Darlene. "We can be the glimmer twins."

"What are you going as, Ti An?" I asked.

"I'm going as a red fox," said Ti An. "I have a beautiful tail."

I brought out my mummy costume to show everybody. "Try it on! Try it on!" shrieked Ti An.

"What do you think Becky's going as?" Lauren asked. I struggled into my long johns wrapped with bandages. I had even painted little drops of blood on them.

"Whatever it is, Becky won't beat your costume," said Darlene. "You look neat."

"Becky says she's not coming," I said.

"Are you disappointed?" teased Darlene. "Nobody to fight with."

"I'm glad!" I said. I took out an elastic bandage and wrapped it around my head, leaving slits for my eyes. I started to walk down the hall stiff-legged with my arms straight out.

"Where are you going?" asked Lauren.

"To . . . my mummy," I said in a deep voice. I wanted to show Mom my costume. I walked downstairs with the Pinecones following me.

Mom pretended to shriek when she saw me. Then she laughed. "You look terrific," she said.

"It's going to be so neat," said Darlene. "I can't wait."

"Would you girls like some lemonade?" asked Mom.

We trooped into the kitchen. "Can you eat in that outfit?" asked Lauren. Lauren was in charge of the refreshments for the party. She had planned ice-cream cake and what she called witches' brew. "It's really just apple juice and club soda," she admitted.

I sat down at the kitchen table and pulled the elastic bandage away from my mouth so that I could eat. No problem.

"Jodi, you make the cutest mummy," said Mom as she brought over a plate of cookies.

"Thanks, mummy. It takes one to know one," I said, scarfing down one of Mom's homemade chocolate chip cookies.

We finished the lemonade and then went back upstairs to go over the final assignments for the party.

"Wait a minute, gang," I said. "I have to go to the bathroom."

I went into the bathroom. And that's when I discovered my fatal error. It was impossible to go to the bathroom in my costume.

I was too tightly wrapped.

I came back out. "Emergency! Emergency!" I cried. I explained my problem to the Pinecones.

They started laughing hysterically. Some friends.

Finally Darlene took pity on me and started unwrapping the bandages so that I could get out.

"What am I going to do?" I wailed. "It's an all-night party. I can't get totally unwrapped every time I have to go to the bathroom."

"Go to the bathroom now," said Darlene. "We'll think of something."

When I came back, Darlene and Cindi were examining the ends of my mummy wrappings.

"I'm pretty stupid, aren't I?" I admitted. "*Now* what am I going to do for a costume?"

"Don't you have two-piece long johns?" asked Darlene.

I hit my forehead with my palm. "Sure. I should have thought of that."

I rummaged in my drawers and came out with my two-piece long johns.

Then I sank down on my bed in despair. "I'll never get it done. It took me nearly a week to sew all those bandages on. They need to be sewed on so I don't come unwrapped doing gymnastics."

"Give me a needle and thread," said Darlene. "It might have taken you all week, but that was by yourself."

"Get five needles," said Lauren. "We can all help."

It was amazing. With all the Pinecones working together, we remade my costume in just a couple of hours. It had taken me days to do it myself.

And the best thing of all was that not once during the two hours did anyone mention Becky.

It's incredible what we Pinecones can do when we put our minds to it.

13

Who Am I?

The gym looked terrific. We had hung orange and black crepe paper streamers from the ceiling. There were about twenty-five kids, a few from Becky's elite group, and a lot from the group underneath us. But I had to say the Pinecones looked the best.

Lauren looked hilarious as a hot dog. Darlene and Cindi certainly were the most glamorous. Well, to tell the truth, Cindi's tutu was a little silly-looking. I can see why her brothers called her a fruitcake. She wore pink tights underneath the tutu, and she looked like a cartoon of a ballerina.

Ti An looked the sweetest. She wore red long johns and a bushy red tail with a white tip. She had the cutest little fox mask that covered only her eyes.

Patrick's sister, who was helping as chaperon, came as Little Bo Peep. She said it was appropriate because Patrick had put her in charge of the littlest kids.

Everybody said my costume was the scariest and funniest. But Patrick had the best costume of all. He came as Count Dracula, the king of the vampires. He wore black tights, a red bow tie around his neck, and a beautiful black cape lined in red satin. He had sewn black bat wings onto the cape.

Patrick has thick curly hair, but he had put gel on it so that it stuck out in punk spikes, and he had white chalk dust on his face.

"I think you win the prize for best costume," I told him. Patrick bowed to me. "You make a mighty mean mummy yourself."

"Why did you pick a vampire?" asked Ti An, giggling.

Patrick laughed. "Don't you know that all great gymnastics coaches come from Romania? You've all heard of Bela Karolyi. I'm just letting my true heritage out." Patrick chomped his fangs up and down.

Ti An pretended to be scared and hid behind me. "Hiding behind your mummy, eh?" said Patrick with a sinister cackle.

71

Fangs and all, Patrick looked incredibly handsome. He was a lot more glamorous than even Darlene. She was wearing cowboy boots and a sequined cowgirl shirt over a pleated cheerleading skirt. Darlene's pom-poms kept shedding.

Ashley had come as a ballerina, too, and she didn't like having the same costume as Cindi. "Mine is a *real* tutu," bragged Ashley. "I played one of the sugarplum fairies in the *Nutcracker* at my ballet recital."

"Mine is a *real* tutu, too," said Cindi.

"It looks like it was bought at a garage sale," said Ashley.

"How did she know?" Cindi asked me.

I laughed. "Don't worry about her," I said. I looked around the gym. Patrick clapped his hands. "As your host, I want to introduce myself. I am Count Bela, the Vampire of Gymnastics."

Cindi put two fingers in her mouth and let out a piercing whistle. Her brothers taught her how to do that.

We all started clapping and whistling.

"And now," shouted Patrick, "let the Monster Bash begin!"

Suddenly Patrick swung up onto the rings and flew through the air. He looked like something from a movie about a vampire. He did an iron cross, a move on the rings that requires tremendous strength. He looked amazing hanging from the rings with his arms straight out and his wings quivering on his back.

Then he did a somersault dismount.

We hooted and hollered our appreciation. Patrick swept off his cape, and then he mounted the high bar.

In men's gymnastics, they use only one high bar, instead of the uneven bars. Mom had told me that in college the high bar had been Patrick's best event. We really never get to see Patrick perform, except in bits and pieces when he's showing us how to do something. He put on a wonderful show. He took incredible risks, releasing high above the bar and then catching it, but he always looked like he was in control. For the first time I understood what he meant when he said "slow down to speed up." Patrick was whipping around the high bar, but when he released the bar and paused in midair, he made it seem like he had all the time in the world to catch it again. I knew in my head that gravity was pulling him down the same way it did the rest of us, but he looked like a creature, half-man, half-bat, who could defy gravity and really fly.

"He's awesome," whispered Darlene.

"This is so neat," said Lauren. "And to think, it was all your idea."

Patrick did a double somersault as his dismount. He was breathing hard.

He bowed to us all.

"More! More!" I yelled.

"Greedy gymnasts," joked Patrick.

But he didn't stop. He hopped onto the beam and pretended to lose his balance.

"Okay," he said. "I have the first game of our Halloween night. Who am I?"

Patrick pirouetted on the beam. He wobbled all over the place, and as he did he let out little hoots. His pirouette was lousy, but he finished with a beautiful flourish with his hands, pointing dramatically into the air.

"Darlene!" yelled Cindi. She was absolutely right. Patrick had mimicked Darlene's melodramatic mannerisms on the beam completely. Darlene laughed.

"Now who am I?" asked Patrick. He pretended to be fussing with his tights as he got ready to do a cartwheel on the beam. " 'Patrick, you're not watching me!' " he whined. " 'I did it perfect and you missed it the last time. Watch me!' "

"Ashley!" I shouted out.

Ashley giggled.

" 'It's a proven fact that I'm gonna fall,' " said Patrick as he imitated Lauren getting ready to do a forward roll on the beam. Lauren started laughing so hard she almost split her hot dog bun.

"Now who am I?" said Patrick. He got Cindi's look of incredible concentration on the beam, and then he imitated Cindi collapsing in giggles whenever she does anything wrong.

Then Patrick straightened up and started to do a series of leaps across the beam. They were funny-looking leaps. " 'Okay . . . okay . . . don't worry. I'm not gonna foul up this time. No way do I need a spot. Don't worry. I can do it alone. I can do it alone. Oh, it makes me so mad when I can't do it.' "

"JODI!" hollered all the Pinecones in unison. I couldn't help laughing. I guess I really did sound that way sometimes.

"Another one. Another one!" shouted someone across the room.

Patrick tossed his head back and forth in an arrogant manner. He pretended to fluff out his curls. " 'Are you watching?' " he asked in a high voice. " 'Because I don't want to do it twice.' "

Then he did a beautiful aerial cartwheel on the beam. It's an incredibly hard move, and there's only one person besides Patrick at the Evergreen Gymnastics Academy who can do an aerial cartwheel on the beam.

Becky.

But when Patrick finished his imitation, nobody laughed.

14

An Overactive
Imagination

"I can't believe she really didn't show up," I said to Darlene. "Don't you think it's amazing?" Until the last minute I had believed that somehow Becky would manage to appear.

"It's terrific," said Darlene. "Now we don't have to worry about anything. We can just party."

I looked around the gym at everybody laughing and having a great time. "I don't know," I said. "How am I going to win my bet if she's not here?" I hated to admit it, but I almost missed Becky. The party was a success, but without being able to rub Becky's nose in it, I felt as if something were missing.

"Every single person will sign a petition that you threw a great party," said Darlene. "Don't worry about it. It's better that she's not here. It's twice as fun."

"When do we do the haunted gym? When do we do the haunted gym?" shrieked Ti An.

"Come on, Jodi," said Ashley. "You said we were going to have terrific games. So far, all we've had is Patrick."

I smiled to myself. Did I have some surprises in store for her! I stood up on the three-tiered podium we use to give out medals during competitions.

"Goblins, ghosts, vampires, ballerinas, and other assorted guests," I yelled. "One by one, I will lead you blindfolded through the scariest gym in the world. Who will volunteer to be the first victim?"

"Me! Me!" shrieked Ashley, hopping up and down.

"Okay, twinkle-toes," I said. "You're first." Patrick took the other gymnasts into one corner of the gym behind some crash mats, so that they couldn't see what we had planned.

I blindfolded Ashley.

"You will now walk the plank," I said, as I guided her up onto the beam.

I held Ashley's hand as she walked blindfolded along the beam. "Uh-oh," I said. "I think one of the witches left a toad's heart sitting on the beam." Darlene was strategically placed underneath the beam with wet sponges. Ashley's foot squashed down on one of the sponges.

"Yuk! It's disgusting," screeched Ashley, but I could tell she was loving every moment of it.

"You have reached the end of the plank," I told Ashley as she reached the end. "You will now have to jump!"

Ashley jumped on command. Cindi and Lauren held onto a huge trash bag filled with cooked spaghetti (Patrick had vetoed the tomato sauce as too messy).

"You have fallen into the guts of the gymnasts who have gone before you," said Darlene. Ashley picked herself out of the trash bag. She had strings of pasta hanging from her tutu. "My costume!" she wailed.

"It's got spaghetti straps," said Darlene, giggling.

I led Ashley over to the floor mats where we had set up a tent that Cindi's family used for camping. It could sleep six and was big enough for even an adult to stand up inside. We had turned it into a little tent of horrors.

"Now it's time for you to go alone into the unknown . . . into the tent of the ghosts of gymnasts past . . ." I said to Ashley as I undid her blindfold. "You must enter the tent alone, as other gymnasts have done before you. There is a treasure for you to retrieve. But beware. There are traps everywhere."

I sent Ashley into the tent and pressed on the switch of my cassette recorder with the tape of spooky sounds, creaking doors, and rattling chains.

The tent was dark, but I had planted a Day Glo skeleton in one corner and there was a slit in the tent through which I could shine my flashlight to make the skeleton glow. I listened to Ashley shriek when she saw the skeleton.

I had also hidden a Halloween present for each gymnast in the tent. I had found tiny little boxes that looked like pirates' treasure chests. They were filled with chocolate candy. I had painted the tops of the boxes with Day Glo paint, and rigged a black light on the top of the tent. When Ashley reached for the treasure, she released a fishing line with a wet sponge on it that hit her in the face.

"Oh, neat," I heard Ashley say from within the tent. I knew she had found the treasure. I held my breath.

Ashley must have reached for the treasure. I heard the squishy sound of the sponge. "Help!" screamed Ashley. Then she started laughing.

Ashley came out of the tent, looking a little foolish. She had the pirate's treasure in her hand

and her hair was streaked with water.

"That was outstanding," she admitted. "Do I get to keep the treasure?"

I nodded.

"It's really cool in there," Ashley said. I glowed. How I wished Becky could have heard her! But if Becky had been there, Ashley would never have admitted how much fun she was having. All in all, Darlene was right. It was great that Becky wasn't there. It was a lot more fun without her.

We took every gymnast through the routine. Ti An was the last one.

I blindfolded her and took her up on the beam. She screamed and almost fell off the beam when I told her that the sponge she was stepping on was the heart of a toad. But Ti An was a good sport when she jumped into the trash bag of spaghetti.

She giggled as I undid her blindfold and told her that I was sending her alone into the haunted tent. I gave her the spiel about finding the treasure.

I pushed Ti An through the flap into the tent. I turned on the sounds of spooky noises.

Seconds later, Ti An ran screaming out of the tent. She grabbed me.

I laughed. "Did the skeleton scare you?" I asked.

Ti An shook her head.

Darlene, Cindi, and Lauren had finished with the beam, and they came over to the tent.

"What's up?" asked Cindi.

"I think our haunted tent was a little too much for Ti An," I said. I could feel Ti An really shaking. "It's okay," I said. "There's nothing really spooky in there."

"Did she get the sponge in the face?" asked Ashley. The other gymnasts had come out to join us.

"Is anything wrong?" asked Patrick.

I shook my head. "Ti An just got a little scared," I said. "But she's okay."

"It was the ghost," said Ti An in a shaky voice.

"There is no ghost, is there?" asked Lauren. "There's the skeleton and the treasure and the spooky sounds. No ghost."

"A ghost. It was a ghost, and it somersaulted right into me and knocked me down," insisted Ti An.

Darlene looked at me. "Did you add a surprise?" she asked.

"No," I said.

"Ti An's just a scaredy-cat," said Ashley.

"She is not," I said. "She was braver than you were on the beam."

Patrick's sister came up with the other little kids. "Isn't it time for the refreshments?" she asked.

"Yeah!" said Lauren.

Everybody rushed to the other side of the gym, where Patrick had set up the refreshments.

Ti An stayed by my side. "Something white tumbled into me," she whispered.

I went over to the bench where I had left my knapsack. I dug out my flashlight.

"Come on," I said to Ti An. "I'll go in with you." Ti An and I crawled under the tent flap. I shone my flashlight on the skeleton. In the beam of the flashlight, it definitely looked plastic and not very scary.

I showed Ti An how to pick up her pirate's treasure and duck when the swinging sponge came down. Ti An giggled. I shone my flashlight into all four corners of the tent. There was no ghost.

"Come on," I said to Ti An. "Let's go get ice cream and cake."

"But I swear I saw a ghost," said Ti An.

I just grinned at her. Ti An is just a little kid. I put it down to an overactive imagination. "When I was eight I used to think I saw ghosts on Halloween night, too," I explained.

Ti An looked doubtful. "Maybe," she said. "But my ghost did an awfully good somersault."

15

Howling Gymnasts

I was tired. I unwrapped my mummy bandages from around my face. I noticed that everybody else had taken off their masks, too. A lot of kids looked bushed, but everybody looked happy, and that made me feel terrific.

After we finished our ice cream and cake, Patrick blew on his whistle. Everybody quieted down.

"I think we all have to agree that this has been an incredible party. There is one person who really deserves our thanks. Let's hear an Evergreen hip, hip, hooray for Jodi Sutton and all her hard work."

I blushed. "Look! The mummy's turning pink," said Darlene.

"Hip, hip, hooray for Jodi!" shouted Patrick. Everybody joined in. Occasionally I had heard people cheer for me when I did gymnastics, but this was different. I had really given everybody a good time.

The Pinecones came up and gave me a hug.

"If only Becky were here," said Lauren. "She'd have a paper bag over her head."

I laughed. Becky not being there didn't bother me now. I really felt good about myself. Maybe Mom was right. Having a good time was the best revenge.

"We should give another hip, hip, hooray to my committee of Pinecones," I said. "They did a lot of work, too." After we gave another round of cheers, Patrick held up his hand.

"Now," he said, "the real test begins. It's getting late. I know you all brought your sleeping bags. I'd like you to put them out on the mats. I want you to settle down. In the morning, we'll have a little dawn gymnastics."

Everybody groaned.

Patrick laughed. "Only kidding. My sister is going out and getting everybody Egg McMuffins for breakfast. Okay, everybody, let's settle down."

Patrick helped us lay out our sleeping bags. All of the Pinecones chose mats along the wall next to our "haunted tent."

84

"We could sleep in the tent," I said.

Cindi clamped her fingers on her nose. "No way," she said. "All my brothers have slept in that tent. It gets to stink after a while, and you can't breathe. We're much better off out here."

I ended up sleeping in between Ti An and Darlene.

"Good night, gymnasts," said Patrick. "My sister and I will be camping upstairs in my office. I want it quiet down here."

Patrick turned off the lights. The gym didn't get completely dark. The lights from the Evergreen Mall's parking lot shone through the windows. It looked a little spooky.

"I can't sleep," whispered Ti An. "This is scary."

"Don't be silly," I said, even though I had been thinking the same thoughts.

You could hear kids whispering and giggling. Then all of a sudden someone across the room started to make small howling noises.

"Shhh," I said.

The howling noises got louder. I sat up in my sleeping bag and swung my flashlight across the room.

It was Ashley. "I'm the howling gymnast," she said.

"Be quiet," I warned her. "Patrick told us to settle down."

"Since when are you such a goody-goody?" giggled Ashley.

Someone else joined Ashley in the howling. It was pretty funny, I had to admit.

Patrick came back down and flicked on the lights.

"Who's howling?" he demanded.

Ashley giggled and burrowed down into her sleeping bag.

Patrick sighed. "Jodi, where are you?" he asked.

"Over here," I said, sitting up in my sleeping bag.

"Girls," said Patrick, "it's been a wonderful night. But now I expect you all to get some sleep. Jodi has done a terrific job so far, so I'm putting her in charge of keeping the noise down in here. I'm serious — I want no more howling. We've had our fill of spooky happenings. Fun is fun. Now it's time to go to sleep. Do you understand?"

"Yes, Patrick," said Ashley in her goody-goody voice.

"What about the rest of you?" asked Patrick.

"Yes, Patrick," we all said in unison.

Patrick laughed. "Good night, everybody. Happy Halloween."

"Happy Halloween," Darlene whispered to me as we settled back down into our sleeping bags.

"Congratulations, champ. You really pulled it off."

"I did, didn't I?" I said contently. I snuggled deep inside my down bag. I was really glowing. Twice Patrick had told me what a good job I had done.

The gym quieted down pretty quickly. It still looked a little spooky to me.

Ti An was lying beside me, her eyes wide open.

"Go to sleep," I said.

"I can't," said Ti An. "I'm still scared. I bet I never get to sleep."

"There's nothing to be scared of," I assured her.

"Will you guys keep quiet?" said Darlene.

Ti An moved her sleeping bag a little closer to mine. I didn't mind. Soon I could hear her breathing deeply on one side of me, and Darlene almost snoring on the other. It was me who was wide awake.

Then my eyes snapped open. The gym was dark. From inside the tent came a low, groaning noise. Slowly but surely, the groaning got louder.

16

The Pinecones Meet the Ghost

"Jodi!" Ti An, suddenly awake again, whispered urgently. "Did you hear that?"

"It's nothing," I whispered back. "Don't wake anybody up."

Darlene rolled over in her sleeping bag. She put her hands over her head. "Too late," Darlene muttered. "Ti An, stop making groaning noises."

"It's not me," whispered Ti An, sounding terrified.

"Jodi, you left the tape recorder on," mumbled Cindi. She sounded half-asleep.

Lauren sat up in her sleeping bag. "What's that noise?" she asked.

The groans and moans continued coming from the tent.

"What's going on?" whispered someone across the room.

"Nothing to worry about," I whispered hoarsely.

Darlene finally sat up. "It's got to be your silly tape of spooky noises. Turn it off!"

I shone my flashlight on my cassette player, which I had put by my sleeping bag. It definitely wasn't playing. The sounds were coming from inside the tent.

"Who's making those sounds, then?" whispered Cindi.

"Or what?" asked Lauren in a fake scary voice.

Unfortunately Ti An took her seriously. "It's the ghost," said Ti An.

"Ti An, you're driving me crazy," said Darlene.

Whatever it was inside the tent chose that moment to make a low, terrible-sounding groan.

"They're back," murmured Ashley, imitating the advertisement for the movie *Poltergeist II*.

The sounds got louder.

I climbed out of my sleeping bag and grabbed my flashlight.

"Where are you going?" asked Darlene.

"I've got to count noses," I said. "Maybe it's one of the other kids doing it."

"I'll come with you," said Darlene. Together we went around the gym, checking each sleeping bag.

Everyone was snug and safe. A couple of kids woke up and wanted to know what was going on.

"Nothing to worry about," I repeated.

Darlene and I walked back to our side of the gym and joined the other Pinecones. The groans were still coming from the tent.

"Maybe we should get Patrick," suggested Darlene, looking sideways toward the tent.

I shook my head. "He told us all to settle down. He put me in charge. I'll go into the tent and investigate."

"Maybe it's Patrick himself," said Cindi. "He could be playing a last Halloween joke on us."

I listened to the groans coming from the tent. "I don't think it's Patrick's kind of joke," I said.

"I'll go with you," said Cindi.

"Me, too," said Darlene.

"Me three," said Lauren.

"Okay, the four Pinecones meet the ghost," I said. I started to open the tent flap.

"Wait a minute," whispered Ti An. "I'm not staying out here by myself." Ti An shuffled out of her sleeping bag. She grabbed my hand.

I pushed open the tent flap and crawled into

the tent. I started to shine my flashlight into the corner. Suddenly something that glowed in the dark came tumbling right at me. It knocked the flashlight out of my hand.

Ti An ducked behind me. "The ghost! The ghost!" she screamed. I put my hand over her mouth.

"What was it?" asked Lauren.

"I don't know," I admitted. I could hear heavy breathing in the tent, but I wasn't sure whether it was us or the ghost.

"I think it's Patrick," said Cindi.

"Look!" said Darlene. The black light flicked on. Something was dressed in a Day Glo leotard and a glowing mask. It did a back flip.

"It's good," I admitted.

"Hee, hee, my little wimps," said the ghost in a weird voice that I didn't recognize. "You will be my slaves."

"That doesn't sound like Patrick," conceded Cindi.

"Maybe we should talk to it," I said.

"I'm not talking to no ghost," said Lauren, who almost always speaks perfect English.

"It's not a real ghost," I said.

"I know," said Lauren, but she took a step backwards. "But it's not one of us, and it's not Patrick. I'm not talking to it."

"Yo, ghost!" I said. "What do you want?"

"I want your youngest gymnast," said the ghost in a deep spooky voice.

"Yipes! That's me!" cried Ti An. I could feel her quivering next to me. The ghost gave an unearthly cackle.

"It sounds more like a witch than a ghost," I muttered.

"I want to go home!" wailed Ti An.

"Let's just get out of the tent," I said. We backed out of the tent. "I've got a plan," I said. "We'll all go back in. You'll get the ghost's attention, and I'll circle behind it."

"How are we supposed to get its attention?" asked Lauren. She actually sounded a little scared.

"Ask it questions about itself," I said. "This is one ghost that loves to brag."

"What?" exclaimed Cindi.

"Oh," said Darlene, looking at me as if she understood.

Lauren did a slow double take. "Oh, I get it," she said.

I nodded. "Keep *it* talking," I whispered. "I'll circle around it."

"This is just like the movies," whispered Lauren.

"How many movies have you seen with a bragging ghost?" I asked her.

"Not many," admitted Lauren.

"What are you going to do when you catch it?" asked Darlene.

"Kill it," I said.

Darlene's jaw dropped open.

"Only kidding," I said grimly. Then I dropped down to the floor and started to crawl on my belly toward the ghost.

17

Who Is the Fairest Ghost of Them All?

"So tell me, ghost," said Darlene in a conversational voice. "Where did you learn such a sensational back flip?"

"I am a natural," intoned the ghost in a deep voice.

"Natural troublemaker," I muttered under my breath. I think the ghost heard me. It cocked its weird-looking head in my direction. I stopped crawling and held my breath. My bandages from my mummy costume almost matched the color of the tent's sides, and I was counting on the fact that in the darkness, the ghost would not be able to see me moving toward it.

Luckily Lauren had the wit to remember what

I had said about asking the ghost questions about itself.

"Ghost, ghost, are you a her or a him?" asked Lauren.

"I am the queen," said the ghost.

Lauren giggled.

"You think that's funny!" snarled the ghost. "I will teach you to laugh at the ghost."

"I only laughed because I was nervous, O Queen," said Lauren quickly.

The ghost threw its shoulders back in a familiar gesture.

"Ghost, ghost, who is the fairest in the gym?" asked Darlene.

"I am!" said the ghost.

I was now just a few feet from the ghost. I rocked back on my heels. I knew I would have only one chance. Either I'd reach the ghost with one leap or I would look like an idiot.

I was about to jump up, when a little voice inside my head started sounding like Patrick. I could hear him saying, "Explosive power doesn't come just from strength. It comes from your head."

Slow down to speed up, I told myself.

"All right, wimps," said the ghost in a nasty voice. "I've waited long enough. Now you will see my destructive power." The ghost reached up. It had a light metal pole in its hand, and it was stretching for the top of the tent. One swipe and the ghost would bring the tent down on all of us.

I sprung like a panther. I tackled the ghost around the waist and threw it onto the mats.

It wrestled me onto my back. It was stronger than I was, but I had the element of surprise on my side.

I turned the ghost over and grabbed for its head. It was wearing a knitted ski mask that had been dipped in Day Glo paint.

I got my fingers under the neck of the mask.

"Wait! Wait! Jodi, don't strangle it!" shouted Darlene. Darlene was shining the flashlight right into my eyes.

The ghost made a mewing noise beneath me. I wondered if maybe I was sitting on it too hard.

I pulled at the mask and ripped it off the ghost's head.

"Jodi!" said Darlene urgently. "Don't do anything stupid."

I took a deep breath. "Hi, there, Becky," I said in a pleasant voice.

18

Temper, Temper

I grabbed the metal pole from Becky. "What was she going to do with it?" Ti An asked. She still sounded scared.

"She wanted to bring the tent down," I said. "That would have caused a mini-riot. Patrick would have come down and been furious with us. He would have thought one of us did it, and she would have snuck away in the confusion. That's what she did when she tumbled into you before. Everyone was wearing costumes. She could just sneak in and out of the tent at will."

"This tent stinks," said Becky. "I can't wait to get out of it. And now you'll be wearing a paper bag over your head," she said. "Even though you caught me, I win. . . . I heard Patrick say he didn't want to be disturbed. If you go to him now and tattle, I win my bet. Patrick may be mad at me, but he'll be mad at you, too. If you don't go to him, I win anyhow. I ruined the party for the Pinecones and especially for you, Jodi. You didn't want me here, and I came."

Becky looked so smug. I half stood up. I wanted to bop her one.

Darlene dragged me back down onto the mats. "I vote we take her to Patrick anyhow," she said. "We can't let her get away with it."

"Me, too," said Cindi. "Patrick will finally see Becky for the sneak that she is. She told everybody she thought Jodi's idea was too joo-vi-nile, and then she came slinking in here 'cause she couldn't bear to miss it."

"Cindi's right," said Lauren. "I say, we march right up to Patrick. Pronto. Let's go."

I sat cross-legged, playing with the bandages on my mummy costume.

"No," I said.

"NO?!" exclaimed Lauren. "What do you mean, no?"

"We're not going to Patrick," I said. "Patrick told me to keep everything under control down here, and I'm going to do it. Becky's going to sleep in the tent, and in the morning she's going to tell Patrick that the reason she snuck in was because she didn't want to miss the most wonderful Halloween party of all time."

Becky snorted at me. "You'll never get me to say those words."

"Want to bet?" I asked.

"How are you going to make me?" taunted Becky.

The Pinecones all looked at me. I knew they all thought I was going to lose my temper and bop her on the nose. But I didn't. I smiled sweetly at Becky.

Becky looked at me suspiciously. "Why are you smiling?" she asked.

"Because you have a short memory," I said. "I'm not scatterbrained like you are. I'm the one who's responsible. I remember when I make promises."

Becky glared at me.

"Jodi, what are you talking about?" asked Darlene.

"This is between Becky and me," I said. "Leave us alone."

The other Pinecones stared at me. "Go on," I said. "We're not going to kill each other."

"Are you sure?" asked Darlene.

"Don't worry," I said. And I meant it. The other Pinecones filed out of the tent, leaving me alone with Becky.

Becky glared at me warily. "You don't really think I'm going to tell Patrick I wanted to come to your party. In front of all the other gymnasts!"

"I do," I said calmly.

"After I told everybody that your party was stupid and that I wouldn't come. I'll look like a fool."

"That's right," I said in the same sweet voice. It was kind of fun being the calm one. Becky just got angrier and angrier.

"You think you can beat me up and make me say it!" Becky was practically snarling.

I shook my head. "I'm not going to beat you up."

"How come you don't sound mad?" she asked suspiciously.

"Because . . ." I said. "Do you remember shaking hands with me in Patrick's office?"

Becky nodded.

I grinned at her. "You promised Patrick in private that you wouldn't do anything to sabotage the party. I promised I wouldn't lose my temper with you. How do you think Patrick's going to like it when he finds out that I kept my end of the bargain, and you welshed on yours?"

Becky shut her mouth and bit her lip. "I was sure you'd have a temper tantrum when you found me here," she said.

"But I didn't," I said. "And you look like you're about to."

Becky looked like she was going to have a conniption, but what choice did she have? I had kept my cool and won my bet at the same time.

I lifted up the flap to the tent. "Sleep tight, Becky," I said in a sugary voice.

"I don't want to sleep alone in this smelly tent," whined Becky.

"Too bad," I said. "You should have thought of that sooner."

Then I paused. I came back into the center of the tent.

"I knew you'd change your mind," said Becky, standing up. "You don't have the guts to make me stay in here all night."

I got out the paper bag I had hidden in my knapsack.

"Here," I said. "It's your costume for the morning."

"How did you happen to have that in your knapsack if you thought I wasn't going to show up?"

"I knew you'd show up. You couldn't miss the party of the century," I said in the most good-natured voice I could muster. I could tell that my good temper was killing Becky.

Then I lowered the tent flap.

I left her alone in the tent to stew.

The Pinecones were all waiting for me outside the tent. "How come we didn't hear screams and punching?" asked Lauren.

"No need for them," I said, as I snuggled back

into my sleeping bag. "Let's go to sleep."

"And just leave Becky alone in the tent?" demanded Cindi. "No punishment?"

"Ignore her," I said, as I rolled over. "That's the best punishment for Becky."

"You know what?" Darlene whispered to me as we fell asleep.

"What?" I asked.

"You're getting awfully smart all of a sudden."

"Well, responsibility brings wisdom," I said.

Darlene rolled her eyes toward the ceiling. "You don't have to turn into an angel."

I giggled. "If I do, I'm sure the Pinecones will bring me back down to earth, right?"

"Right," said Cindi and Lauren, who had been listening to every word.

19

A Bet's a Bet

Darlene nudged me. I groaned. It felt like we had just gone to sleep. I looked at my watch. It was only six forty-five A.M., but Patrick was standing in the middle of the gym, surveying the damage. The little kids across the gym were already up. His sister was handing out breakfast.

"Good morning, goblins, witches, ghosts, ballerinas, and mummies," said Patrick.

I sat up in my sleeping bag. The gym looked a sorry sight with the orange and black crepe paper drooping from the ceiling.

"Congratulations, all of you. You were a lot quieter than I expected."

Just then Becky poked her head out of the tent

flap. I grinned. She was wearing a paper bag over her head.

"Who's this?" asked Patrick.

"It's Becky," I said.

Patrick looked perplexed. He walked over to the tent. "I thought you said you weren't coming to the party."

Becky's voice sounded peculiar coming from the paper bag, but her words were music to my ears. "I didn't want to miss Jodi's party," she said.

The Pinecones started to giggle quietly.

"Are you saying that I pulled off a *great* party?" I asked the paper bag, in a loud voice.

"The greatest," muttered Becky from underneath her paper bag. "I would have been an idiot to miss it."

The Pinecones started laughing so hard, they were hooting. Soon the whole gym was in hysterics.

"Uh, Becky," said Patrick. "I'm about to serve breakfast to everybody. Don't you want to take that paper bag off your head?"

"No, thank you," said Becky.

"Is she going to wear that paper bag on her head all day?" Lauren asked me.

"She's the one who made the bet, not me," I said. "She won't starve. I made a hole for a big mouth. I knew Becky would put her foot in it."

The Pinecones started laughing again.

A little bit later, I was helping Patrick clean up the gym. Patrick held the dustpan while I swept some of the crepe paper into it.

"By the way, Jodi," said Patrick. "I want to congratulate you again on a job well done."

"Thanks," I said proudly.

"I particularly liked the way you tackled the uninvited ghost," he said softly.

I almost dropped my broom. "You saw?" I exclaimed.

Patrick shook his head. "I didn't see. I heard." He pointed to a metal grill right above us. "My office is right over the tent," he said. "The only heat I get up there is from a vent. I didn't mean to eavesdrop, but these old concrete buildings have weird acoustics. I can even hear whispers."

"So you knew Becky had snuck in," I said. "She was going to try to scare all of us and throw the party into a riot."

"She must have made you mad," said Patrick. "I thought about coming down myself, but I wanted to see how you'd handle it. I couldn't have handled it better myself. You know, Jodi, it might not be what you want to be, but someday you could make a great coach. You're good at handling a crisis."

"Me?" I started to exclaim. I thought about all the things I would normally say, that I'm too scatterbrained, that I hate responsibility, that I'd always lose my temper. But then I stopped. None of those things was really, really true.

"Can a mummy be a coach?" I asked Patrick.

"Why not?" said Patrick. "Yours is."

I laughed. Then I looked across the room. Becky was eating her Egg McMuffin through the hole in the paper bag over her head.

Patrick followed my eyes. He shook his head.

Darlene, Cindi, and Lauren came over to me. "What was Patrick talking to you about?" Darlene asked.

"Next year's Halloween party," I said.

Darlene looked across the room at Becky. "Are you going to let Becky take off that paper bag?" she asked.

"No way," I said. "Listen, maybe I learned to control my temper, but a bet's a bet. Besides, I'm beginning to like the way she looks."